MARTHA

Martha Stinks!

Adaptation by Karen Barss

Based on a TV series teleplay written by Karen Barss

Based on the characters created by Susan Meddaugh

HOUGHTON MIFFLIN HARCOURT

Boston • New York

Martha Speaks
Picture Clue Key

Dad

Martha

diaper

meat

dishes

refrigerator

friends

socks

Helen

trash

house

For information about permission to reproduce selections from this book, write to Permissions, Houghton Mifflin Harcourt, 215 Park Avenue South, New York, NY 10003.

ISBN: 978-0-544-09662-2 hardcover | ISBN: 978-0-544-10012-1 paperback

Design by Rachel Newborn

www.hmhbooks.com | www.marthathetalkingdog.com

Manufactured in China
SCP 10 9 8 7 6 5 4 3 2 1
4500420087

There is a bad smell in the .

"What stinks?" 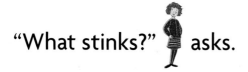 asks.

Is it the dirty ?

Is it Dad's ?

Is it Jake's  ?

Is it the  ?

What *is* that smell?

Soon they find out!

", you smell!" says.

"Do you like it?" asks.

"We rolled in !"

"No. You stink!" says.

"Bath time for both of you!"

But  will not take a bath.

She is sent out of the  .

Skits takes a bath.

 misses  .

But  is too dirty to come in the .

"We need a plan, Skits,"  says.

" and will not agree."

 has an idea.

She calls her .

She asks to help her at the park.

Skits tells  about free at the park.

The hold a dog wash at the park.

 arrives.

"Where's the free ?" asks.

Then, 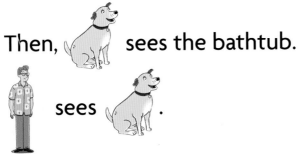 sees the bathtub.

sees .

"It's bath time,  " says.

"I am a dog. Dogs like to stink!" says.

"If you want to come in the ,
you need a bath."

"We miss you!" says.

"I'm ready for a bath," says.

"Sleeping outside stinks!"

Martha Speaks
Smells Great to Me!

Sometimes Martha and Helen do not agree about what smells good. See if you can match Martha to her favorite scents and Helen to hers. Are there any scents they both like to sniff?

Answer key:

Martha likes trash, cake, dog treats, turkey drumsticks, and other dogs.
Helen likes flowers, cake, turkey drumsticks, and soap.

24